THE IRISH AT 97 ORCHARD STREET

FOREWORD

Ruth J. Abram President, Lower East Side Tenement Museum

Many writers have pondered the line between fact and fiction. “Fiction,” opined the playwright Edward Albee, “is fact distilled into truth.” Francis Bacon said, “Truth is so hard to tell, it sometimes needs fiction to make it plausible.” When asked to describe the difference between fiction and reality, the thriller writer Tom Clancy responded, “Fiction has to make sense.” It is because of fiction’s special ability to convey “truth,” that the Tenement Museum turned to the novelist Joseph O’Connor to “make sense” of the narrative of the Meehan-Moore family.

Mr. O’Connor’s treatment of the narrative, more than met the Museum’s expectation that he would make the facts come to life. While O’Connor was writing, the Museum staff was busy developing the apartment.

The Moore family parlor at 97 Orchard Street, as recreated to c. 1869.

It was decided to set the Moore apartment at the moment of the family’s wake for five month old Agnes. The baby’s small white coffin sits in the center of the parlor. Her mother’s chair is carefully placed nearby, witness to the dreadful watch she kept all night long beside her baby’s coffin.

To create an historic immigrant apartment, the Museum first gets the story straight. This is done by gathering all manner of documents. In the case of the Moore family, these included census, bank, and church records, birth and death certificates, naturalization papers, city directories, and newspapers.

Once the narrative is sketched out, it is sent to the Museum's curator who assembles the furnishings to support the story. The furnishings are arranged in an empty apartment, and for over a year, representatives of various groups are invited to view the "mock up" apartment and to discuss the story. In this way, the Museum is able to deepen its interpretation and hone the narrative to reflect contemporary questions and interests.

We invited teenagers to take a look. We asked them if they felt it was inappropriate to present an apartment in which a baby's coffin is so prominently featured. When they learned that 40% of the babies known to have been born at 97 Orchard Street died in childhood, they said that it was very important that we tell that story. They also reported that they themselves were not unfamiliar with death, having among them lost siblings or parents or aunts and uncles, and grandparents. Perhaps this apartment could be the basis for discussions of those losses.

We invited Irish Catholic leaders. In one memorable viewing, they asked whether the Moore's younger daughter, who, unlike her parents and older sister, never learned to read or write was developmentally disabled. When we inquired why they asked, they said that in their tradition, a developmentally disabled child is referred to as one who is "touched," meaning, touched by the hand of God. This signals to parents and the larger community that this child must be understood to be and treated as a blessing.

We invited immigrants who remarked that like the Moore family, they felt they got the short end of the stick when it came to health care. In the case of the Moore family, the problem was bad milk. In their case, it's access to qualified medical practitioners.

We invited physicians to help us understand all the illness and death which marked the Moore family's time at 97 Orchard Street. Examining birth and death certificates, they declared that all members of the family had died from causes with which we no longer contend because of the great dike of public health measures we have erected in America. For instance, the cows' milk given to baby Agnes by her parents was likely to have been tainted with additives such as chalk and ammonia to disguise its color and smell. Today, inspection rules insure poisoned milk can not reach the market. The physicians felt the Museum had an opportunity to use the Moore story as a basis for discussing public health.

The Moore story reminds us how difficult the immigrant experience has been – and continues to be. At the same time, when the Museum tracked down descendants of this couple, it found them serving as teachers, police officers, fire fighters and more. Contributing Americans all, they stand as proof that all the effort exerted by their forebears – and ours – to overcome appalling adversity was worth it. Their story calls us to realize that when the children and grandchildren of contemporary immigrants reflect upon the experiences of their immigrant generation, they will be filled with the same pride and awe with which descendants of Bridget Meehan and Joseph Moore regard them. And they will have every right to do so.

The Moore family kitchen, recreated to how it may have appeared in 1869.

What Might Have Been

Joseph O'Connor

On the landings of the tenement house the women had gathered to pray. They stood in the candlelight, in trios or alone, murmuring litanies to the Blessed Virgin and then to Saint Jude, the patron saint of lost causes. It was an hour before dawn. When their candle burned out, they prayed in the quarter-light for Agnes.

VATER UNSER IM HIMMEL,
GEHEILIGT WERDE DEIN NAME...

Bridget Moore could hear their supplications as she wept by the little one's cradle, wiping the infant's forehead, clasping her emaciated hands. They were praying in their German dialects and, as other women came to join them, in the Latin words that united all those of their faith: in the *Aves* Bridget had learned in her girlhood in Ireland, in *Glorias* and *Credos* and heartfelt *Pater Nosters*. It was springtime in New York; only three weeks after Easter. The trees were leafed out. Her child was dying.

Her husband had fetched an ice block from a *bierkeller* on Ludlow, had hammered it down to chunks which he wrapped in a fold of old muslin, so that the child could be cooled and her fever assuaged, for he had convinced himself there might be hope in coolness. His hammerings had awakened Mary Catherine and little Jennie, Kate aged four, her sister only two. He had bawled at fretful Kate to get out, *get out*. Bridget Moore had beseeched him to go easy.

“Cough Balsam; Benjamin Sperling, Prescription Pharmacist; 257 Broome St., Cor. Orchard St. New York” This patent medicine bottle was discovered in apartment 15 at 97 Orchard Street.

It was April the 21st, 1869. Bridget Moore was in her twenty-fourth year. All the night long she had kept watch in the tiny, cramped kitchen, with its acrid redolence of sickness arising from the cradle, and the odor of scorched chimney soot from the empty grate, and its print of the Sacred Heart.

Joseph had watched along with her almost until the dawn, exhausted by the effort of having walked the streets for hours, searching for a doctor who would come to a tenement. They had no money left to pay.

Dr. Topping appeared weary; he was doctor to the poor. He had on a yellowed nightgown beneath his heavy frieze raincloak; of late, the city's nights had been cold. He had barely looked at the child before pronouncing the case hopeless. The patent cure that they had purchased would not heal her, he said. Nothing would heal her. It was scrofula, and "wasting." "Marasmus" was the medical term. There was nothing he could do. She was simply too feeble to live.

They could dose her with alcohol, if they had any, for the pain. She would be dead by morning, he told them. In his two decades of practice he had uttered many such verdicts; they had never grown easy to say. Joseph Moore had answered that perhaps the doctor was incorrect; surely there was something that could be attempted to save her. She was only five months old. She could not be permitted to die. Bridget Moore had said nothing, as though never having had any faith in doctors; as though wondering why he had been summoned at all.

The sun rose slowly on the ghettoes and mansions, reddening, then silvering the rivers of Manhattan, and reddening, then silvering the windows of the slums, and coaxing loamy smells from the earth. The birds in their nests gave small, bright shrieks. Tugboats stirred on the Hudson. At dawn Bridget Moore could hear the rasping croak of a rooster, and the quarrelling of a Bavarian couple from somewhere downstairs, and from lower in the house the slam of a heavy door as a plumber went out to his work. Joseph had nodded unconscious on a backless chair by the stove, with Jennie face down and asleep across his knees, and Kate, thumb in mouth, clutching a poppet he had made for her, asleep in the crook of his arm. There was water on the floorboards where the ice had melted.

His clothing was soaked. He was barefoot. Bridget Moore woke her husband to say he was needed now. It was important to be brave; she needed him.

He had watched, weeping silently, as though ashamed to be weeping, while Agnes Mary Moore, the youngest of his three children, had died in her mother's embrace.

Through the flimsy walls of their home, in which they had lived only a few months, the bereft couple heard the Lord's Prayer being offered. It rose in its volume and sharpened in its pitch, as though the women on the landings knew the terrible thing that had happened. The Irish couple inside had lost their tiny daughter. The little ones had lost their sister.

DEIN REICH KOMME,
DEIN WILLE GESCHEHE,
WIE IM HIMMEL, SO AUF ERDEN...

In the years to come Bridget Moore would remember this moment, picturing it from the vantage of her child's departing spirit, as it gazed down sadly on the rooftops of *Kleindeutschland*, on the steeples and palaces and meadowlands of Manhattan, on the synagogues and sweatshops, on the gridded-out streets which diminish in size, blurring into one another, as she neared to the homeland of Heaven. But that is a picture for the years to come. This morning there are no such pictures.

Then the women on the landings heard the pierce of Kate's weeping, for at four she was old enough to understand what was told her by her parents: that the baby had gone away to Paradise now, where Lord Jesus would mind her in his love. She would suffer no more. She would cry no more. A priest from the cathedral arrived.

The priest from the cathedral was young, still shockable. He begged forgiveness for having come to them so late. He, like Bridget Moore, had been awake all night, for six others of his parishioners had been close to death that night, and there were not sufficient priests to see all of them. He had never been to this house, its quarters crammed with immigrants, its single creaking water-pump for the use of twenty families. There were worse tenements, he knew, in the Five Points and elsewhere: slums of abject misery where lives were short and cruel and everything you touched seemed to stink of death and loss. This house was at least new: a step up for its tenants.

Filigree crucifix with tripod legs, c.1860-1880, on display in the Moore apartment at 97 Orchard Street. Nineteenth century newspapers like the *Irish American* contained numerous advertisements for stores in Lower Manhattan that sold Catholic religious items.

But this one he would never forget.

He believed in the God who had walked with the poor, preaching the holiness of hunger, the sanctity of the forgotten. He prayed by the body of Agnes Mary Moore, that ruined and deserted house.

Neighborwomen came in and took Kate and Jennie to their apartments, to mind them an hour and to feed them and hold them; to share what little they had with these children whose parents had been struck by the unimaginable fate. Then two others came in, quietly as a rumor, an older woman and her sister, born a long way overseas, to wash the child's body and prepare her for burial, for Bridget Moore, they felt, could not be asked to do such a thing. She was too young herself to be asked.

A ribbon of black crepe was pinned on the door, with a card bearing the name and age of the dead child, which a neighbor had written in lines of black ink, for he felt it was the only solidarity he could offer. He had been born in rural Ireland, had seen many die in the Famine: buried in pit-graves, unremembered, dumped, disposed of like beasts by the wealthy who ruled them, and he would not see a child disrespected. The women washed Agnes Moore, and placed candles by her body, which they dressed in the linen robe in which she and her sisters had been baptized. The undertaker, Mr. Hart, brought a coffin so small that he could carry it unassisted up the staircases of the tenement. It was white, as was the custom when the deceased was a child. Joseph Moore could not watch the entrance to his home of such an object. The priest helped Mr. Hart with his work.

James Kennedy, a mason who lived downstairs, knocked quietly and came in to condole. One of the few Irish neighbors in this dwelling-house of immigrants, he was a decent man; quiet, sober in his habits. It was said that he had a wife someplace but nobody knew where, nor even if the stories of his marriage were true, for often they contradicted one another. He spoke to Joseph and Bridget with his brown eyes lowered, as though afraid to confront their grief in the dazzle of its recentness. They were barely able to reply.

“Funeral in Baxter Street,” detail, *Frank Leslie’s Illustrated Newspaper*, 1865

A coffin for my child. A casket small and white. How can such a conversation be happening? You do not bury your child. Your child buries you. As though all of it was a fever-dream from which Bridget Moore might awake, to the street-sounds and rhythms of another day in New York, and the cry of a baby for the mouthful of milk that the rich might give to a cat.

There are moments, late at night, when Bridget remembers her life in Ireland. The stillness of the lanes. The smell of wet turf. The faces of the old people as they talked of the past, of pieties and weather and local events; and the sound of Gaelic being spoken. A cartwheel on the wall of a blacksmith's forge. Her uncles at work on the bog. A long time has passed since she last stood in a field in Ireland, or walked the familiar thoroughfares of an Irish town. Dead wasps in the windows of the sleepy little stores. Soldiers in red coats. Beggars. Ploughboys. The sea air apple-crisp, as though you could take bites out of it. A ruined, ivied monastery where foxes now live.

Onward she walks, through the cacophony of Orchard Street, past peddlers and stallholders, through clusters of hawkers, past the windows of Schubert's butcher shop, past the little German beer hall where carters are unloading clanking crates. Memories blur like the spokes of a wheel. It was another life, her seventeen years in Ireland. A girlhood that seems far away.

Embrittled, scooped out, she walks as in a dream. Her eyes are tired and sore from tears. Strange languages swirl around her like flutters of streamers: the tongues of Saxony, Bavaria, Prussia; of other lands across the sea. Faraway places and wandering peoples. The smells of strange food. Spices she cannot name. From the embrasure of a window comes the sound of rabbinical singing, for a boy who loves Jehovah lives in that room. And there, on the corner of Stanton and Essex, stands the little Florentine peddler, with his ribbons and combs. This city with its hundreds of thousands of immigrants, its parlances, its music, its impenetrable slangs, its countless deities, its ghettoes and rookeries, has nothing to say to her grief. A black woman is selling strawberries: people say she was once a slave. Everyone in this neighborhood has a story behind them. So does Bridget, now.

The woman whose infant daughter died this morning, who prayed and hoped to the last wrenching moment. She walks slowly, heavily, through the windblown dust, traversing the busy and dung-smirched streets, for there is a funeral to be arranged and Joseph is too broken to do it. This time yesterday morning his daughter was alive. Sick, yes; but life means hope. He will not go to the chapel, says he cannot face the priests, for he would be

“Distributing Coal to the Poor in Cherry Street,” *Harper’s Weekly Magazine*, 1877.

afraid of the things he might say to them. He wants nothing of God. *There is no God now*. It is Bridget who goes to the chapel.

Her husband does not like her to talk about Ireland. That is all in the past, Joseph says. It's the Irishman's trouble in this country, he insists. The Irishman won't forget. He'll keep holding on. If only he'd assimilate, he'd be running the United States today, instead of being walked on by these Know-Nothing Yanks. "The past is an anchor," Bridget Moore tells her husband. A proverb of her mother's from home in Ireland. "Anchors weigh you low," says Joseph dismissively. What is done is done: his creed.

The ship is part of her memory, but it disconcerts him when she talks of it. He asks her not to speak of it before the children. It would only upset them, so Joseph insists. There is no need to go talking of such distressing matters. She knows nothing of his own voyage except that it started in Dublin. Asked once by little Kate how he had come to New York, Joseph had winked at his curious questioner: "I swam it," he said. "Then I flew like a seagull. Your Papa got all sorts of queer trickeries, so he does. Your Papa got wings you can't see, girl."

"Mama says she came in a boat. And the people was hungry."

"That's only a story. She don't mean it."

Bridget walks on. The ship tilts in her mind. The mind is an ocean, fathomless, turbulent, with eyeless things in its depths. She had watched the coastal mountains of Ireland recede, wondering to herself were there mountains in New York. The flap of the mainsail: fricative, like wings. The creaking and groaning of age-old timbers. She will never forget the terrors of that passage. Long ago the ship had been used to transport slaves: it was said among the passengers that the lower deck was haunted, that a cry could be heard near the fo'castle at night and that if you heard that eerie and terrible cry, your death by morning was certain. You would be buried at sea, without stone to mark you. There were sharks in the chasms of the Atlantic.

Pier 17 and Fulton Ferry at South Street, date unknown.

A night in a storm when the billows struck so hard that the ship was almost beam-ended and every glass on board was smashed. Three weeks of seasickness but, worse, the lack of privacy. Even the women without the slightest privacy. Then the blessed smell of the land: the green fields of Brooklyn. The sight of a farmer in his pasture near Red Hook, waving his hat in greeting

as the ship drifted coastward. Around him, his milk-cows, their udders fat and heavy. He has seemed to Bridget Meehan an angel of America. The passengers were singing a hymn.

AGNES BEATAE VIRGINIS
NATALIS EST, QUO SPIRITUM
CAELO REFUDIT DEBITUM
PIO SACRATA SANGUINE...

She enters the church. It is cool and dark. Candles burning lowly before the statues of the martyrs. The odor of beeswax and incense. The rich, heavy wood of the serried lines of benches, and the purple of a confessional curtain. And high in the rafters, the carved faces of men and women, cut there by the boatwrights who fashioned the timberwork on the corbels. The images of their people back in Ireland, it is said. And one of those graven, imperturbable faces has always reminded Bridget Moore of an uncle back in Ireland who went away one autumn to pick a harvest in England and never came back to the townland. She looks up at the rafters through the mote-filled beam of light. Her grief is like a swallowing of ice.

Built in 1815, Old Saint Patrick's Cathedral was a center of Catholic religious life in 19th century New York. On November 8, 1868, Agnes Mary Moore was baptized in the Cathedral by Father James McGean.

It was here in this church, on a bright winter Sunday, that she first saw Joseph Moore. He had been kneeling beside another man; she watched them going up to receive. His eyes met hers as he returned to the pew. There was a brazenness about him, an assuredness she liked. He was not like the boys back in Ireland. The next Sunday morning he had introduced himself on the porch. He had a flower in his hand. He gave it to her.

If your people were around you at a time like this. Your mother and father. All those you grew up with. Her own mother lost children, has walked that painful road. If your mother were here, it would help you. Saint Agnes. "The lamb" in the language of her faith. And *Agnus Dei:* the lamb of God, who died and resurrected to the life eternal. Who conquered death by love.

A wreath of withering lilies on a plinth before a plaque for the Irish boys who died in the war. The fighting Irish. Heroes of Gettysburg. Joseph has no time for "all that auld talk." They want the Irish to build their roads for them, fight their wars, kill their Indians, whose land was robbed off them for nothing, he says. Then get soused and die quiet in some gin-shop, he says. And that's the Yanks' plan for the Irish. The way the Americans talk, you'd swear no Irishman ever did anything bar shooting someone innocent and spouting the rosary. He likes being mischievous. It's one of the reasons she loves him. He sees the world differently. His own man.

America was at war when she came to New York. Recruiting officers were gathered on the dock. She had watched some of the boys sign up to fight, as though joining some brotherhood of revellers on a spree. Not a minute in America, still staggering with sea-legs, pucking one another on the shoulders, saucer-eyed with excitement. A boy she had fancied, Michael English from Ennis, had led two of his cousins to the tent in Castle Gardens and asked the Yankee sergeant for a uniform and a gun, for he was ready to prove himself in the country of liberty. 'Tis a tiger you're looking at here, boss.' It had seemed strange to Bridget Meehan — to come all this way in the hope of a new life, only to fight in another man's war.

She did not understand the war, its causes, its purposes. Joseph had tried to explain it to her, but she suspected he did not fully understand it either. The whites of the South wanted to be free of the North. They wanted to own slaves, he said.

"But they don't truly own them, the way you'd own a cow or a beast."

"They do," he said. "That's the way of the South. They auction the Negro on the block like a beast."

"But all men are free in America,' she said.
"Not the Negro," he said. "He ain't free."

"Ain't," said Joseph Moore, and she thought he said it proudly, as though displaying his allegiance to his adopted city. His eyes were sea-green, and they glittered like new coins. He loved New York. He would make himself a home here. His hope was to make that home in a German neighborhood, for Germans were industrious; good strong Americans, serious, optimistic, who didn't sing of the old country, who never looked back but always forward. His children would be Americans. It was the greatest country on Earth. Sometimes he spoke in contradictions.

She drifts up the shadowy aisle and asks dazedly to see the priest. She is Mrs. Moore, she tells the aged nun who is dressing the altar. Mrs. Joseph Moore of Orchard Street; mother of Agnes. Yes, little Agnes Moore, who died this morning. The funeral. Yes. The nun nods.

There is a wedding in progress in the chapel near the transept. The party is small, no more than half a dozen guests, but the bride and groom, who look nervous and excited, are an affecting sight to those watching. Two elderly women observe them, taken by the spectacle. "Go *halain*," one of them says. The Gaelic words for "beautiful." A memory of her own wedding arises in Bridget's mind while she waits for the priest to come to her.

Joseph had looked so princely as he waited on the steps of the church, with his cousin smoking furiously, as though he were the one getting married. It was not the ceremony itself she tended to remember; not the words of the priest, nor the prayers, nor even the vows. It was the way he had looked at her from outside the chapel. An expression of such kindness, of hopefulness and courage. It was the moment they had married, so it seemed to Bridget Moore, the instant when she knew he would always care for her. "I thought you wouldn't come," he had joked to his bride. "I nearly didn't," she had said. And he had laughed.

He was always laughing. Always had a joke. "When I first met my Bridget," he used to tell everyone, "there was straightaway an attraction. A powerful attraction." He would pause a moment or two before adding, archly: "And before too long, I felt the same way." His gaiety was a kind of currency.

"I am sorry for your trouble, Bridget," Father Hanahoe murmurs. He is an old man, born in Sligo; Bridget Meehan has washed his clothes. She takes in the priests' laundry; it earns a little extra for the family. She keeps some of the money back to send to her mother in Ireland. She suspects Joseph knows, but he silently permits it. Her parents at home need help, he knows. You cannot forget where you came from.

Now she weeps, wishing not to, wiping her tears with her thumbs. Father Hanahoe will say the requiem for Agnes. An old man, courtly, who has seen many mothers weep, and she tries to swallow her tears, but she cannot. And if only Father Hanahoe would take her in his arms, but he cannot, for a priest would not be permitted to do that; and so he must watch the rawness of her pain as it spills and streams from her eyes. And the bride and the groom, alerted by her quietly echoing sobbing, turn from the side-altar and stare a little resentfully.

"Courage," whispers the priest. "Be strong. Your children need you. Be certain that you have an angel in Paradise this morning. We are promised that, Bridget. Have not the smallest doubt. It is hard for you now, for you are sharing in the cross. But Agnes is sharing in the resurrection."

The child needed milk, she wants to tell the priest. Perhaps I didn't give her enough. We had so little to spare. Or perhaps it was gone bad. I don't know what to think. I don't know what to do. Do you think it is my fault? Was there something I could have done? The money I sent to Ireland? Should I not have sent money to Ireland? My mother and father have nothing to eat. Should I not have sent the money to Ireland?

Rosary with wooden beads, c. 1860-1870, on display in the Moore apartment at 97 Orchard Street

Some days she walks over to Mott Street, where she and Joseph lived as newlyweds. Mary-Kate was born there. There had been happy times. The neighborhood was rowdy, full of toughs and low gin-shops, and at night you could hear raucous singing from the den across the street, and once— Joseph denied it, told her she had too much of an imagination — the *pok pok* of gunshots from an alley near the shambles. But there was love in that cell of a room she had shared with her husband. It had seemed a consolation, a protective shell. The fictions we believe when we are young.

A married woman. She would silently repeat the phrase to herself, as she walked the astonishing streets of Five Points. Through the grit and the cinders and the turmoiling flies, by the rancid open sewers and wild-eyed dogs. Past the watching eyes of corner-boys and hardscrabble gangmen. By the gaze of penniless women, burnished hard and cold by hunger, who had crossed half a world to find plenty and peace but had found only newer kinds of want.

Nothing can touch me. I am married now. She had believed it as an article of faith.

Joseph, a Dubliner, was warm-hearted, handsome. He worked as a waiter in hotels in the season; he would also do saloon work: he worked hard. He knew all of the Irish ward bosses; they liked him, assisted him, though in truth he had little interest in politics. All he wanted, he told her, was work; a chance. To be allowed to make a home for his children.

He had a Dubliner's sense of himself; his endless possibilities. He disliked the maudlin ballads the drinkers would sing, of old Irish place names, half forgotten love affairs. *Fare thee well, Eniskillen, fare thee well for a while... I wish I was in Carrickfergus...' Tis far away I am today, from scenes I roamed a boy.* He'd chuckle about the singers. He'd say they were looking back over their shoulders. It was "rawmashe" they were singing, a Gaelic word for trash-talk. "What use was Ireland to me or mine?" he'd say. "It's well out of it we are. I'd rain bombs on it if I could. England can keep it; matter a damn to me, girl, for Ireland don't grease no pan."

"A Tenement in Mulberry Street," *Harper's Weekly Magazine*, 1873

That shabby room in Mott Street. Their palace, he used to laugh. In the tenements of Dublin, they'd have to share it with another family. He had seen pitiful things in Dublin, that nobody would believe. Children in prostitution. Old people abandoned to beg. The poor were as nothing in the teeming, filthy hovels. But that was in the past. Before America.

They spatted about it sometimes; her feelings about Ireland. He was not an angry man but he could be impatient, truculent, his edginess fuelled, so Bridget often felt, by a sense he had of time being an enemy to the poor. What irked him most was when she said, as she sometimes did, that she dreamed of one day seeing Ireland again, that it would be a blessing for the children, and for her family back home. "It's me and them girls is your family now," he would say. "Wish to God you'd quit your dreaming, for it only leads to sadness. You'd want to wake up, girl, and look at where you are. Ireland's only a stain on a map."

Joseph took a drink, but he wasn't a drunkard. He'd seen what drink did. He didn't like it. You work in a city's barrooms, you see too much of heartbreak. The hard luck story and the good man ruined. He'd take a bottle of porter of an evening at home, but he didn't touch whiskey: that was trouble. And then, when the first of their children was born, he had taken a pledge never to drink again. His way of thanking God for such a blessing, she knew, though he always denied it, saying her head was in the clouds. Sometimes he missed Mass. He rarely went to confession. Religion was for women, he said. But one night she had found him on his knees by Mary Kate's cradle, praying in a whisper; it had shocked her to hear his words.

I'm begging you. If you're there.
Don't let anything ever happen to my child.
I'm begging you. Blessed Jesus, have mercy.

Sleigh-style cradle with spindle sides, c. 1850, on display in the Moore apartment. This style of cradle was popular with mid 19th century reformers because its open sides allowed air to circulate around the sleeping baby

My child will be buried in New York City, and I will never see my mother again. Far in the future, in decades, in centuries, the body of my child will be part of New York City. And I, myself, will always be here now. I will never see my mother again.

The funeral is to be held tomorrow, for in cases such as these, a longer period of mourning is unwise, said Mr. Hart. He speaks with the practiced diplomacy of his profession, in euphemisms, sidelong looks; sometimes in silences. Flowers would be useful to have in the room. Lilies, if possible, for their smell is sweet and heavy. Better for the casket to be closed, Mrs. Moore. When the deceased was so young, and also so very thin. And he is silent, as though guilty for something.

Even though there is so little time, she consents that there should be a wake. For some reason, it seems important to Joseph. She watches as he drapes the mirror in the parlor, the way the people back in Ireland prepare for a waking; for at the hard time of life an old way can seem important, the way you might mock at the easier time. The few dollars he has managed to raise at the pawnshop on Grand Street are spent on food and drink for the visiting mourners. There must also be tobacco, Joseph insists. A wake must be done with propriety.

Is he trying to help her? Does he think it is what she wants? Or somehow does he want it himself? He borrows chairs from some of the Germans, places them carefully about the room, neatly, efficiently, like a waiter preparing a function, never once looking at the terrible object in the corner. His face is slick with sweat.

They file in to the parlor quietly, as though trespassing on a privacy, the women clutching rosary beads, the men with hats in hand. It is as though they are waiting for something to happen: some sacrament, perhaps, or simply a revelation produced by their solidarity, their sitting together in a room. Some of the callers are neighbors, others she does not know. Men from the bar where Joseph works, she assumes, for they all seem to know him, they greet him quietly by name. Dockers, stevedores, navvies: all Irish, and a man who is an organizer of some sort for the Democratic Party, and another, from the Ancient Order of Hibernians, who have offered a little money towards the funeral. And others who insist on speaking to her in Gaelic, as though the sound of the old language could heal. And the German women come in, speaking lowly in their own languages, which she does not understand, so replying is impossible, or in broken phrases of English, or saying nothing at all, but sadly shaking their heads and touching her hand. But it hurts her to be condoled with, for there is nothing to say, no matter the language or the kindness lying behind it. She wishes they would all go away. They sit together in the room, the women around the coffin, the men in a group by the doorway.

That is not a body. That is my child. Why are all these people in my home?

Candles burn down. The visitors speak quietly. The child, she is told, has gone to a better place. A place where there is no suffering, where the poor are loved and honored. It is how her elderly parents used to talk about America. A land of honey. Of milk.

And she recalls the waking held for her on her last night at home. Her father and mother and the gathering of neighbors. A drover singing a ballad in a corner of the cabin and then a fiddler came in, but he wasn't good. "Get up with me, Bridget," said her father, late in the night, "and face me in a step. Will you do that for me, girl? For likely it's the last dance we'll ever have in the world." And she and her father had danced in the kitchen. And in the morning she had left for the port, for the ship, with a couple of shillings and an address in New York: an agency placing Irish girls as domestic servants in the houses of the wealthy of Manhattan.

Dear Mother. She imagines the letter, as more mourners arrive. Tobacco smoke purples the air. Bridget Moore cannot write, and her mother cannot read, but Joseph sometimes helps his wife to write a letter, and someone back in Ireland — the schoolmaster, she thinks — helps her mother understand the news from New York. So it will be the voice of the elderly schoolmaster, whose name Bridget Moore cannot now remember, that will pronounce the terrible words of the letter: that Agnes Mary Moore, who lived only five months, has lost her life in New York.

My child is dead. Why can't you understand? There is nothing you can say to me now.

Honor Frawley, an old Connemara woman who lives on Elizabeth Street, comes into the apartment clad in a ragged black shawl. Leather-faced, black-eyed, something Spanish about her. She bends to kiss the tiny coffin and immediately begins a keening: a soft ululation, wordless at first, but soon settling into the *ochons* and *brons* of Gaelic. The German women stare at her. Some of them look frightened. From outside in the street rise the cries of the vendors, then a bawled obscenity, and the rattle of a cart. Rain spatters on the windows. The room is too full. The children are restless on the floor.

And the letter cannot be written by Joseph, she knows, because that would be to ask him to relive what has happened. She will have to seek the help of somebody else. A neighborwoman, maybe. One of the priests at the church. She does not realize that what has happened will be recollected every day, for the remainder of her life, for the remainder of Joseph's, that mourning is not what happens on the day of a funeral, but in the months and the years to come. Grief comes in instants, in memories and desires, long after the mourners have departed the room. It is carried in the senses, in the body itself, that each of us inhabits alone. Around the corpse of a child stand a multitude of ghosts: the child herself, the child's own children, the lovers unmet, the friends unmade, the dreams undreamed, the hopes annulled, and the ghosts of the parents, now living in a world where the sacred rules have been shattered. They will see an infant in the street, or hear a baby's squalling cry, or smell the miraculous aroma of a newborn's precious head, and be speared, in that moment, by all that might have been, had only a child been permitted life. They will know the amputation of such a grief as this. There will be nights when they feel like orphans.

He stands by the doorway, in a suit that does not fit him, which he borrowed from Mr. Solomons, a tailor on Delancey. The shirt collar is too tight; its pressure is reddening his face. He looks hollow-eyed, close to tears, but he will not weep. He would never weep in public; he thinks it unmanly, and she is glad that he thinks this, for she could not bear to see it. She has dreams in which their bed is a raft in strong seas. The creaking of its quoins is the wind.

He moves among the mourners, offering drinks and plates of food as though waiting the plentiful tables at the hotel where he works. There are murmurs among the German women that the landlord should come to pay his respects, or at least send his wife, as though any of that would matter, but someone keeps translating the murmurs to Bridget, and she looks across the parlor at her husband. It is only when the rosary begins that his shoulders start to quiver, and quietly he departs the room. But she cannot leave the room. The children need her presence. A woman has no other choice than to stay.

Once, in the summer of her first year in New York, when she was working as a housemaid for a family on Washington Square, she had paused while shining the silverware in their beautiful parlor to look at some of the magazines on their card table. She could not read English well but she recognized the word IRISH under a cartoon of a leering, ape-like man with a cudgel in one paw and a bottle in the other, and two filthy, decrepit crones by his side. Was that how the family thought of her? An ape-woman of Ireland? Was that how her like would forever be seen in the land of the brave and the free?

And another time, at night, when she was walking home from Mass, a soldier had approached in the street making drunken propositions. He would pay her a dollar. Two if she pleased him well.

"I'm an honest girl," she had said. "You'll not talk to me so."

"You're a nigger blanched white," the soldier had scoffed. "That's all you'll ever be here, girl."

Joseph had told her not to speak of it. America was a good country. There were oafs and louts in every land on God's earth. We'd be better not to mind them or to give them any credence. It was shortly before they were married.

"The eight-hour movement. A group of working men on a strike in one of the uptown wards," detail, *Frank Leslie's Illustrated Newspaper*, 1872

My dear Mother,

I write with hard news and do not know how to say it. Our little daughter Agnes died on Wednesday the twenty-first, and was buried in Calvary Cemetery. Our hearts are broken. There is nothing I can tell you. The priest says I am to say my prayers to the Holy Virgin, and I do say my prayers — but they do not help me.

My husband would not let go of the coffin when the time came for to bury her, only standing by the graveside and destroyed with his tears. The good of his life is gone, and I am afraid for him now. Mama, say a prayer for us. How I long to be at home. I would give anything to see you, anything in the world.

I wish you could have seen her for she was a beautiful looking child and every time I looked on her I thought of you and Daddo.

I enclose four dollars and hope it might be of use to you.

Pray for us. Your loving

Bridget.

Spring turns to summer. Neighbors leave the house, and others, newer immigrants, come to live there. In the basement of the tenement there is a busy German tavern, and at night the crowds of drinkers spill out into the street. She can hear them as she scrubs the priests' old clothes; laundering, mangling, folding, pressing. Washing until her hands grow wrinkled and sore. Hanging cassocks around the rooms like strange weeds.

He gets the moods of an evening. He works too hard. There are nights he comes home from his work after midnight, jaded by the exhaustion of having to be cheerful all night, for a bartender has to stay cheerful, no matter how he feels, no matter his private thoughts or the troubles of his home. Men don't want sullenness in a barkeep, ever. And Joseph doesn't want it in his wife.

He hates working in the saloon but that's all he can get since he was dismissed from his job at the hotel. A drunken diner insulted him. Called him a dirty Irish leech. Told him to get home to the cesspit he came from. There was an angry scene; he was ordered to apologize to his abuser. He would be dismissed if he refused to. He refused to.

He sits silently by the window, staring down into Orchard Street, listening to the drinkers, their shouts and catcalls about girls, or politics, or nothing. You can't approach him any more. Lately he can be bitter. This man, that man: all of them are untrustworthy. The German neighbors don't like us. They hate all the Irish. Call us Tammany thieves. Bogtrotters. Monsters. These Lutherans around here: they all stick to themselves. That Schneider, who manages the bierhaus in the basement — he'd no more employ an Irish than a black man or a Chinese. She tries to point out that the Irish are the same; they will only support their own; but he will not listen. *What chance has a man in a town such as this?* Coming here to New York was the worst mistake he ever made: this is what he says when the blue mood descends on him. Hostilities he doesn't mean. Intolerances he doesn't feel. Opinions he would ridicule if uttered by others. As though his body is emitting a color, she often thinks. He has changed since Agnes died.

Can't you keep them children quiet?... Can't you let me alone?... Can't you get yourself some work?... I am weary, I told you... Can't you make the money last?... No, I don't want to talk... I've been talking all night... I've a pain in my face from talking...
Will you let me alone!... Can't a man sit in his god-damned house?...
Is it out I have to get for some peace?

The city now eludes him, like a friend he'd like to make but he doesn't know the words of introduction. Stories of other men's success in America seem to haunt him. A Sligoman who made a fortune out beyond in San Francisco. A Dubliner who owns a silver mine in the new state of Montana, yielding tens of thousands of dollars a month. A Galwegian born in destitution on a famine ship in the harbor, who now employs hundreds of Irish navvies, and who is building a mansion so opulent and gracious that even the Yanks are envious. She has dreams of Joseph wandering a hall of many doors, opening all of them, one by one, but finding nothing behind. *It's here*, he mutters. *Someplace it's here*. As though the thing he seeks so frantically he already owned, but he lost it, or it was stolen by a burglar.

Once, in the August after Agnes's death, she saw him on the corner of Rivington and Allen, staring at a poster in a store's dirty window:

MEN WANTED FOR NORTHERN CALIFORNIA

it said.

GREAT FORTUNES

To Be Made

IN THE WEST.

Civil War era suitcase, c. 1860-1870, on display in the Moore apartment. The Moores moved every year during their first half-decade in America and may have used a trunk similar to this one.

There was gold in California. Nuggets the size of your head. For a week or two, he had talked about moving out west. Scrape up a few dollars. Wipe the dirt of New York from their feet. *Think of it, Bridget. We'd live like royalty! Get out of this kip, we'd live high on the hog. It's a new start we need, I can see that now. I'd been praying for a guidance and here it is.* Although terrified by the prospect, she had agreed it was a good idea. For she knew all he wanted was someone to agree with him. He has a man's need to be valued, to be listened to, admired. New York does not provide him with that any more. Not since Agnes died.

He borrowed a map from someone. There were pamphlets, gazetteers. Land was available to everyone in the west. The terrible wrench of his feverish enthusiasms, as he plotted how they would get to California. But there was never enough money to save for the journey; they were in arrears for the rent; the children needed food. The plan was quietly forgotten, as though it had never been made, and one night, when they were cold, he burnt the tattered map for kindling, and he left the apartment abruptly, slamming the heavy door behind him, and did not return until it was late.

Whiskey bottles c. 1870-1880. When friends and neighbors came to the Moores' apartment to pay their respects after Agnes' death, Joseph may have offered them a glass of whiskey.

Months turn to seasons. Orchard Street under snow. The mournfully beautiful entreaties and praisings drift out from the synagogue on Norfolk. Christmas comes, and he works longer, harder; in hotels and kitchens and barrooms and cafes; he takes every shift he can find. A busy time of year for a waiter in New York; often, he works sixteen straight hours. And Bridget works harder, and the priests' clothes keep coming, and she sends a few dollars home to Ireland every month: money she can scarcely afford. Her hours, her days, are measured in priestly clothes, in walks to the post office to send money. She buys milk for the children. She will go hungry to buy milk. She begs her two daughters to eat.

The fears for health. The fears of another pregnancy. She and Joseph love their children but it is so hard to make ends meet. There are moments -- yes, it must be admitted -- when she dreads the possibility of having more. Her health is not good. The German women tell her she is grown *totenblass* or *totenbleich*: their words for sickly pale. Lately, climbing the staircases in the house has been harder; she is breathless, swimmy-headed; plagued by strange, powerful hungers, which never alleviate no matter what she eats. And there are days when neither of them eats.

She and Joseph have talked but such conversations are difficult. They embarrass him, she knows. They embarrass her, too. There are certain times, she says, certain weeks of the month, when a man and woman can be together without a child being made. A woman in the house has told her; it is a matter of calendars. Joseph consents, for he could not bear her loss. It would kill him if anything were to happen to her, he says. But they are young, with the longings of the young in love, for the comforts of the body, the escape of that intimacy, and they believe in the God of love, who will protect them, and if a new life is willed by that heavenly ordinance, the sin is in wishing things otherwise.

A new year dawns. A child is growing inside her. Joseph promises that they will manage; the better times are ahead. Their luck will change; it must, he believes, for America is good to the man who works, who is honest and loyal and who stands by his family, who never asks a hand-out, who never begs or steals. It might take a little time for the promise to be made good. But it will be. He believes it. There is no other choice.

"Tenement Life in New York—Ragpickers Court, Mulberry Street," *Harper's Weekly Magazine*, 1879.

She watches the newer immigrants come to the house. She sees them in the courtyard, clustered around the water pump, waiting to use to the single privy the tenement affords, or playing with their children in the smoke-filled air. Some of the men talk of politics, a revolution that will come, when the poor of the whole world will be brothers together, and nations will not matter, and all chains will be broken, and the starvelings will arise from their slumber. They start to seem young to her; a sign that she is aging. She feels for them: these people with their bundles and children. Has anyone ever told them the truth she now knows? That this country of freedom can be cold to the stranger. That to emigrate might well be to shorten your life. There will be poverty, bigotry, the mistrust of the locals, who will mutter that you are lazy, that you bring disease, that you never assimilate, that all your kind are strange, that you do not belong, do not want to belong, only to come here and scrounge off your betters. And through all of it you will work all the hours you are able, and raise children in the hope that their lives will be better than yours. To leave a home and cross the ocean for the sake of a chance. Only a chance. No certainty but that. There are moments when she wonders if it is the land of the free. But it is certainly the home of the brave.

Bridget Meehan and Joseph Moore will never go to California. Nor ever will they leave New York. The merciful immigrant sisters who washed Agnes Moore's body will live many long years in Suffolk Street, Manhattan, until their home is demolished and they take to sleeping in the streets, in the doorways and alleys of the Lower East Side, and they simply disappear from view. Others of the women who assisted that morning will always know hardship in the newfound land, as will many of the men who gathered in that room to stand with their grief-stricken neighbors. Some will die in poverty. Some will scrape a way. Several of their children will serve their city with honor: police officers, firefighters, schoolteachers, workers; one will be a public defender; another a criminal; several will be American soldiers. Jennie Moore will marry. Kate Moore will not. In her teens, Kate will work as a hair weaver to help support her family, Jennie as a maker of paper flowers. James Kennedy, the stonemason, will share his immigrant surname with a President. Many heroes will move through those small, lightless rooms. Some will never leave them.

Bridget and Joseph Moore will move on several times: to Elizabeth Street, a neighborhood of much destitution, where many of the residents are Irish and gruelingly poor, and then to Third Avenue and 28th. Bridget will give birth to five more children. No headstone will ever record their names; but they lived, were loved, were real. Josephine Moore. Elizabeth Moore. Cecilia Moore, who died at seven months. Teresa Moore, who died aged five. And Veronica Moore, who lived only four days, and who rests in Calvary Cemetery with her family. With her mother, who will die at the age of thirty-six, and her father who will live to his seventies. His last move is to 31st Street and Second Avenue, where he resides with his eldest daughter until she dies at the age of forty. His final years are lived alone.

An elderly Irish waiter who is sometimes seen in Orchard Street, late at night in April. He stands by the doorway of a dilapidated tenement that looks as if it should be condemned by the authorities. One time, he left a flower; another, he made the sign of the cross. But mostly he stands for a short time alone, looking up at the windows, unnoticed by passers-by. Nobody knows why he would come here any more. A pale old ghost of a father. He dies in the winter of 1916, the year of the Easter Rising in Ireland. Like his loved ones, Joseph Moore will have no headstone.

"Funeral in Baxter Street," detail, *Frank Leslie's Illustrated Newspaper,* 1865

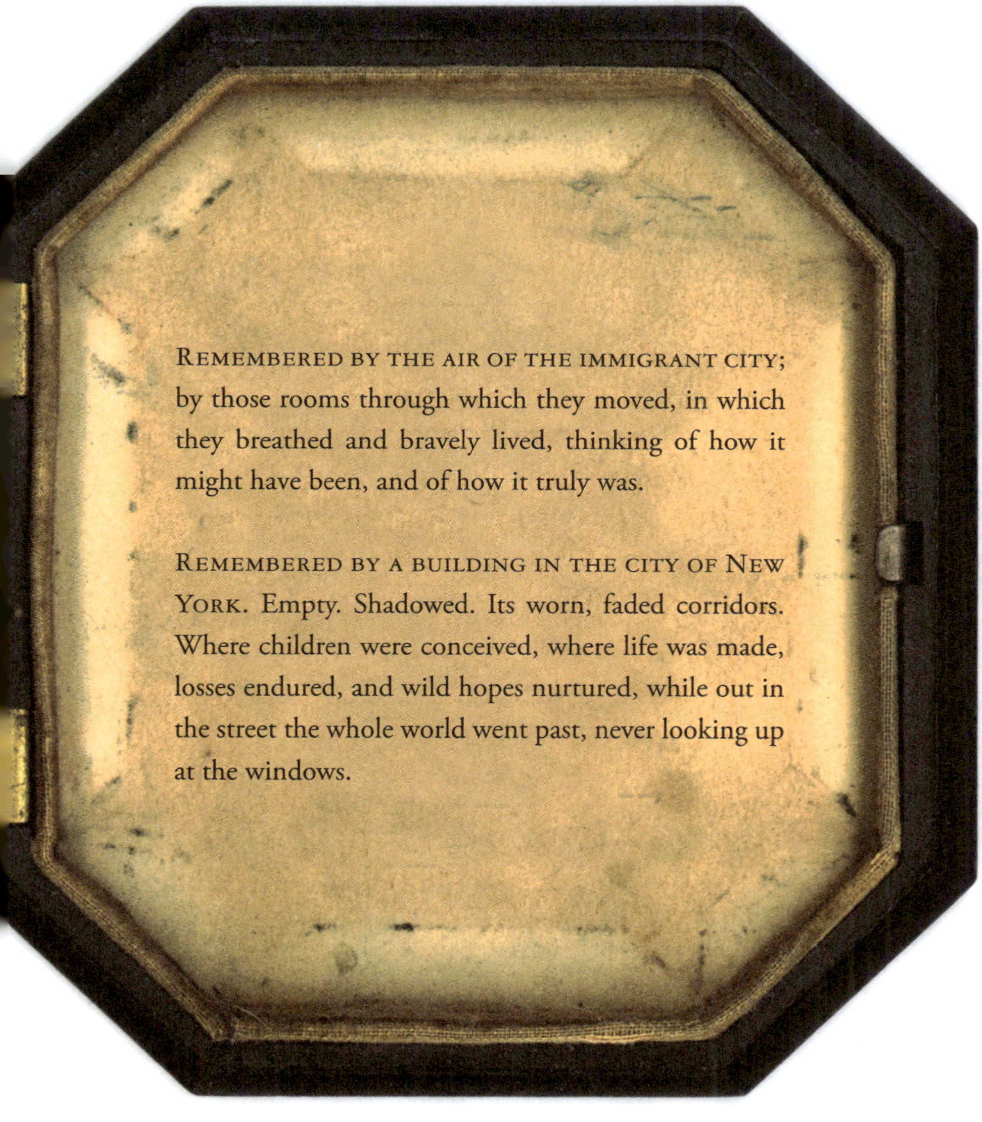

Daguerreotype case, c. 1856–60

REMEMBERED BY THE AIR OF THE IMMIGRANT CITY; by those rooms through which they moved, in which they breathed and bravely lived, thinking of how it might have been, and of how it truly was.

REMEMBERED BY A BUILDING IN THE CITY OF NEW YORK. Empty. Shadowed. Its worn, faded corridors. Where children were conceived, where life was made, losses endured, and wild hopes nurtured, while out in the street the whole world went past, never looking up at the windows.

C M C K E E F F E
M. FITZGERALD
PASSENGER
NEW YORK
STEERAGE

AFTERWORD

The Moore Family and Irish Immigration to New York

Arlene Kirsch, editor

IN 1863, SEVENTEEN-YEAR-OLD Bridget Meehan emigrated alone from Ireland to New York. Joseph Moore arrived two years later in 1865 at the age of twenty. Most likely they met and married in New York sometime during 1865, but Museum researchers have been unable to locate a record of their marriage. It is unclear where in Ireland Bridget hailed from, but records indicate that Joseph emigrated from Dublin. He and his family may well have been Dubliners for generations or, like some residents of Dublin, they may have migrated to the city from a rural county decimated by poverty.

Before she met Joseph, Bridget likely worked as a domestic, a pattern followed by almost half of all Irish immigrant women in 19th century New York. Once Bridget married, she quit her work outside the home, as most Irish women did. Although she is listed in subsequent census records as keeping house, Bridget may well have continued to earn wages, perhaps by taking in laundry.

Throughout the course of his life in New York, Joseph Moore found employment as a waiter and bartender. In the 1880 federal census, he is listed as working as a waiter in a hotel. While Museum researchers are uncertain as to where exactly Joseph worked in New York, he is likely to have been employed in an establishment owned and operated by an Irish proprietor, rather than one run by a German resident.

opposite: "Emigrants Leaving Queenstown for New York," *Harper's Weekly Magazine*, 1874.

***Dan Bryant in the character of Myles Na Coppaleen*, 1865. Bryant was a popular minstrel and music hall figure of the 1850s and 60s.**

Joseph and Bridget's migrations didn't end once they arrived in New York. Like many immigrant families, they moved frequently as their fortunes fell, rose, and fell again. Almost every year they moved to a different building in Lower Manhattan. Within two years of arriving in New York, they were living at 65 Mott Street, in the notorious Five Points neighborhood, among poor Irish, African Americans, Chinese, and a myriad of other ethnic groups. At 65 Mott Street, Bridget gave birth to Mary Catherine Moore, the first of many children. A year later, the family moved to 150 Forsyth Street on the Lower East Side, where Jane Moore was born in 1866 and Agnes Mary Moore on October 31, 1868. Within a few months, they moved just a few blocks east to 97 Orchard Street. The move from Five Points to the three rooms of 97 Orchard Street in Kleindeutschland, a neighborhood of skilled workers and newer tenements, no doubt represented a significant step up for the Moores.

Just after moving to 97 Orchard Street, infant Agnes died of marasmus, a type of malnutrition — the first of many such losses the Moores would endure over the years. Bridget and Joseph lived at 97 Orchard Street for only a year before moving again half a dozen blocks to 224 Elizabeth Street where Bridget became pregnant with another daughter, Cecilia. She bore four more children after Cecilia: Theresa, Veronica, Josephine, and Elizabeth. From Elizabeth Street the family moved to Third Avenue and 28th Street in Murray Hill, where Bridget passed away at age 36 from what the attending physician described as "fatty degeneration of the heart." She had buried Agnes, Theresa, and Veronica by then. Only four of Bridget and Joseph's eight children, Mary, Jane, Josephine, and Elizabeth, survived into adulthood. Agnes was not the only baby to die because of unsanitary conditions. Diptheria, which is frequently linked with overcrowded living conditions, caused Elizabeth's death.

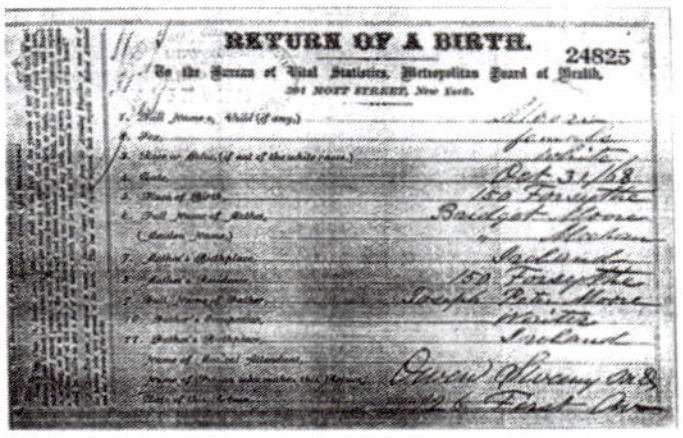
RETURN OF A BIRTH.
24825

Agnes Moore's birth certificate for 150 Forsyth Street, October 31, 1868

opposite: "Homes of the Poor," *Harper's Weekly Magazine*, 1883

By 1880, the Moores' two eldest daughters, Mary and Jane, were contributing to the family economy. Mary, 15, worked as a "hair weaver," and her 13-year-old sister, Jane, worked manufacturing artificial flowers. Mary stayed on with her father until she died in 1907 at the age of 40.

Museum researchers have been unable to determine what became of daughters Josephine and Elizabeth who are last listed as living with Joseph, Mary, and Jane at 519 First Avenue in the 1890 Police Census.

Socioeconomic Status

Compared to the predominantly Irish population of the Sixth Ward's Five Points neighborhood, those Irish who lived at 97 Orchard Street in the Tenth Ward appear to have enjoyed more comfortable quarters and practiced more highly skilled occupations. When, in the course of their first five years in New York, the Moores moved from their first home on 65 Mott Street in the Five Points (purportedly the City's first purpose-built tenement) to the newly constructed 97 Orchard Street in Kleindeutschland, it signified a small measure of the family's upward mobility. While nearly half of all Irish men in New York City during the 1860s and 1870s were employed as unskilled laborers, many of the Irish at 97 Orchard Street found work as clerks, artisans, waiters, or bartenders. One was James Kennedy. According to the City Directory, Kennedy worked as a mason. Charles Dineen, who immigrated in 1861, lived at 97 Orchard Street in 1864–1865 and worked as a clerk in a store

Joseph's final move was to 31st Street and Second Ave, where he lived to the age of 71. Although he is listed as being a naturalized citizen in the 1870 U.S. Census, Joseph's official naturalization papers date from 1874. It could be that he naturalized twice; first fraudulently and later legally. If his first naturalization had been fraudulent and subsequently challenged by Republican officials, Joseph might have needed to naturalize legally in order to vote. During the late 1860s, Tammany Hall perpetrated thousands of fraudulent naturalizations with the intention of mobilizing an army of new voters. According to official records, however, Joseph didn't vote until 1884, when he was living at 519 First Avenue with his four surviving daughters.

In 1895, Jane married Roger Hanrahan, the son of Irish immigrants, in 1895. Roger and Jane had two sons, Raymond and Roger Jr., and three daughters, Estelle, Anastasia, and Frances. By 1920, the family moved to the Richmond Hill section of Queens. Today, their descendants live throughout the country, but some continue to reside here in New York City. One of their great grandsons became a New York City police officer and another worked for the New York City Fire Department.

LITTLE GERMANY

When 97 Orchard Street was constructed in 1863, the surrounding neighborhood was populated mostly by German immigrants. Despite its German majority, the mid-19th century Lower East Side was far from homogeneous. German immigrants mingled with Irish, Italians, Jews, and African Americans. Germany did not become a unified nation until 1871 and the German-speaking residents of the Lower East Side came from thirty different German states with various linguistic, cultural, and religious differences. Although it stood in a section of the Lower East Side known as *Kleindeutschland*, or Little Germany, the building housed several other ethnic groups including the Irish. Between 1863 and 1935, 97 Orchard Street was home to approximately twelve Irish families, among them Joseph and Bridget Moore. In addition to the Moores, Lucas Glockner, the building's first landlord, rented to the Dineens, Sullivans, Murphys, and Byrnes, among others.

The Moores and other Irish neighbors would have encountered Germans and other immigrants in their hallways, on the roof, around the backyard water spigot, and while shopping from street peddlers and in nearby stores.

Jane Anne Hanrahan, *carte de visite* c. 1895. In 1895, Bridget and Joseph Moore's second child, Jane, married Roger Hanrahan, also the child of Irish immigrant

Raymond Hanrahan, *carte de visite* c. 1899. Born in 1898, Raymond was the third child born to Roger and Jane Hanrahan.

"Laundry Day in the Tenements," ***Harper's Weekly Magazine*, 1889**

Socially and religiously, however, Irish, German, and other immigrants most often kept to their own ethnic circles. Germans often belonged to regionally based mutual assistance societies and fraternal lodges or vereine; attended German-speaking churches including the leading German parish, Most Holy Redeemer; and frequented German saloons, beer halls, and wine gardens. The Irish tended to belong to county and other ethnic associations and benefit societies, attend Irish churches, frequent Irish saloons, and support Irish causes.

IRISH IMMIGRATION TO NEW YORK CITY

The mass Irish emigration that began with the Great Famine of the 1840s holds sway over the popular imagination, but Irish migration to the United States dates to at least the 18th century when thousands of mostly Protestant Irish from Ulster County in what is now Northern Ireland made their way across the Atlantic Ocean. Fleeing a homeland troubled by colonial persecution and the destruction of the once flourishing linen and woolen trades, many emigrants landed in New York as a result of the city's extensive commerce with Ireland. By the late 18th century, thousands of Irish immigrants were arriving in New York every year. Some of these Irish, such as the Duanes and Clintons, went on to become prominent and influential in the life of the city, while the majority worked as laborers, tradesmen, and farmers.

In the decades after the Famine, more Irish women than men immigrated to the United States. The Irish were the only significant group of foreign-born in which women outnumbered men and in which women emigrated alone without any family members.

Between 1815 and 1845, well over one million Irish men, women, and children left Ireland, a considerable number of whom landed in New York. In contrast to the Protestant Irish emigrants of the 18th century, those who arrived in New York during the first decades of the 19th century were overwhelmingly Catholic.

Then, in 1845, a catastrophe of epic proportions was visited upon the people of Ireland. A widespread, insidious potato blight, the result of a fungal infestation, devastated the crop throughout the country and robbed the rural poor of their main source of food. Striking Ireland repeatedly between 1846 and 1855, the Great Famine resulted in the deaths of between one and one and a half million Irish from starvation and famine-related diseases. Another two million, one hundred thousand people fled the country, with one and a half million settling in the United States, many in New York City.

"Emigrants on Shipboard," *Every Saturday*, May 6, 1871

"Interior View of the Office at Castle Garden," *Harper's Weekly Magazine*, August 15, 1868.

Those who left Ireland in the late 19th and early 20th centuries enjoyed a more comfortable journey and a more amiable reception in New York than their Famine-era predecessors. By the late 19th century, steamships had reduced the time of the trip from five to two weeks or less and were more comfortable and sanitary than sailing vessels.

The cramped and claustrophobic steerage quarters in which Famine-era emigrants crossed the Atlantic swarmed with disease and "fever." More than nine percent of those who sailed on these "coffin ships" perished on board, some shortly before their arrival. Nonetheless, the Irish who immigrated to the United States between 1846 and 1855 represented the largest mass migration during the 19th century. Once settled in America, these Irish immigrants tended to view themselves as exiles rather than voluntary emigrants, the victims of a forced exodus perpetrated not by the potato blight, but by their English imperial masters.

The largest wave of Irish immigration to North America followed the decade of the Great Famine. Almost half of all Irish immigrants to America since 1700 left their homes in Ireland between 1855 and 1921. Poor harvests, evictions, and collapsing farm prices combined to drive almost three million Irish to leave Ireland for the United States. From the 1870s on, more than half of these emigrants came from the most impoverished regions of Ireland, along its Atlantic seaboard.

Inducements to emigrate also originated on the other side of the Atlantic, as letters and money sent home to Ireland by Irish people in New York were crucial to financing the passage of others. In some cases, remittances came in the form of prepaid passage. Often termed chain migration, one family member journeyed to New York and, once settled, worked to bring the rest of the family over. In addition, brokers and agents of shipping companies, as well as immigrant assistance societies, circulated promotional materials to stimulate emigration.

"Interior of Castle Garden," ***Harper's Weekly Magazine*****, 1871**

Arriving in New York, later Irish immigrants no longer had to navigate a barrage of runners who met them on the dock with the intention of cheating them out of their meager savings. Castle Garden at the southern tip of Manhattan was created by the State of New York in 1855 to process new immigrants and help them make the transition to the United States. There, Irish immigrants could purchase railroad and riverboat tickets, obtain advice from representatives of religious and benevolent societies, and consult employment agencies staffed with translators. After 1892, responsibility for processing arriving

Thousands Are Sailing

You brave Irish people wherever you be,
I pray stand a moment and listen to me;
Your sons and fair daughters,
They are going away,
And thousands are sailing to Amerikay.
So good luck to those people
And safe may they land.
They are leaving their country
For a far distant strand.
They are leaving old Ireland,
No longer can stay,
And thousands are sailing to Amerikay.

Minstrel Boy
The minstrel boy to the war is gone,
In the ranks of death you'll find him;
His father's sword he hath girded on,
And his wild harp slung behind him;
"Land of Song!" cried the warrior bard,
"Tho' all the world betrays thee,
One sword, at least, thy right shall guard,
One faithful harp shall praise thee!"

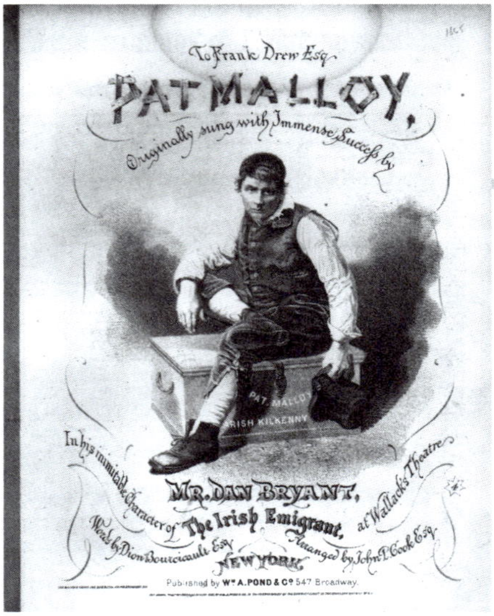

immigrants fell to the Federal Government. Ellis Island in Upper New York Bay became the main point of entry for newly arriving Irish.

THE IMMIGRATION OF IRISH MUSIC

Irish immigrants arrived in New York with a rich musical tradition. For centuries in Ireland, music and song were transmitted orally and performed by itinerant balladeers. Acting as storytellers and community historians, balladeers composed songs narrating the shared experience of colonization, famine, and emigration. Often using existing "airs" or tunes, balladeers typically juxtaposed lyrics, titles, and melodies to create a dynamic musical folklore.

***Pat Malloy,* sheet music, 1865**

***Maggie Murphy's Home,* sheet music, 1890**

***My Father Sould Charcoal,* sheet music, 1868**

Songs sung on both sides of the Atlantic spoke both to the difficult journey faced by Irish immigrants and the lives they hoped to find in America. With remarkable feeling, they seem to convey the ambivalence some emigrants must have felt as they left home in search of a better life thousands of miles away.

Written in 1865 by an unknown author, "Thousands Are Sailing" describes an "American wake." When thousands of young men and women left Ireland for America during the mid-19th century, family and friends held an "American wake" to express their grief and commemorate the passage of an individual out of the community. Traditionally, a wake was held to mourn a deceased friend or family member. But because it was unlikely that emigrants would ever return to Ireland, their departure was as final as death itself. During the American wake, relatives and neighbors held an all-night vigil for the soon-to-depart, alternating prayer and keening with drinking, dancing and games.

In America, music continued to play an important role in the lives of Irish immigrants. Among the most popular songs brought by Irish immigrants to America were those composed by Thomas Moore (1779-1852). Setting words to the melodies of 17th and 18th century Irish harpers, Moore's compositions were widely available in songbooks, broadsides, and sheet music throughout the 19th century. "The Minstrel Boy" is a song written by Moore and set to the melody of the Moreen, a traditional Irish tune. It is widely believed Moore composed the song in remembrance of his friends who had died during the

Irish rebellion of 1798. The song gained widespread popularity and became a favorite of many Irishmen who fought during the American Civil War.

In addition to bringing songs from Ireland, immigrants wrote and performed new compositions chronicling the often difficult experience of negotiating life in what could be a strange new land. The songs of Harrigan and Braham were the popular music of their day– sung in saloons and concert halls around the city. Like a balladeer, Edward Harrigan chronicled immigrant life on the Lower East Side with humor and affection. Sometimes called the "American Dickens," he frequently noted conversations overheard in the city's streets and parks.

Not only did immigrants encounter this music in public venues such as the music hall, the sheet music business helped immigrant families bring these tunes into the home. Written initially for a stage show entitled *Reilly and the 400*, the song "Maggie Murphy's Home" depicts a tenement apartment reverberating with music where "there's an organ in the corner, to give the house a tone." "Oh, bless the leisure hours/ That working people know," the protagonist sings, suggesting that music and dance within the home provided an emotional release from the stress and exhaustion of urban life, creating a space where communal ties were celebrated and reaffirmed.

"Children Dancing to the Music of a Street Musician," *Scribner's Magazine*, 1893.

Irish immigrants in New York often found their experiences reflected in song broadsides posted on buildings, fences, and railings throughout the streets of the city — sometimes in a satirical tone. They might have encountered songs such as "No Irish Need Apply." Like traditional, orally-transmitted ballads, song broadsides took current events as their subject. Available for the price of a penny from street hawkers, newsstands, and stationeries, song broadsides — written to familiar tunes — were a ubiquitous presence in 19th century urban life.

Although America held out the promise of opportunity for 19th century immigrants, many Irish encountered considerable discrimination. Written circa 1865 by John Poole, "No Irish Need Apply" describes the prejudice met by some Irish immigrants in their search for work. Among the best-known Irish-American ballads of the 19th century, it chronicles the historical reality of anti-immigrant nativism and widespread discrimination against Irish immigrants.

Cause of death.	TOTAL DEATHS under 5 years.
Small-pox	146
Measles	275
Scarlatina	753
Diphtheria	241
Croup	381
Whooping-cough	199
Diarrhea	2,638
Cholera Infantum	1,226
Inanition	173
Scrofula	52
Tabes Mesentorica, including marasmus	809
Hydrocephalus	607
Tubercular meningitis	143
Meningitis	574
Encephalitis	96
Convulsions	985
Nismus nascentium	48
Congestion of brain	141
Laringitis	54
Bronchitis	616
Pneumonia	939
Congestion	99
Gastritis	50
Enteritis	222
Gastro-enteritis	183
Jaundice	33
Premature birth	375
Preternatural birth	32
Cyanosis	90
Atelectasis pulmonum	119
Malformation	43
Hemorrhage	14
Atrophy	32
Astehenia debility	102
Total of 34 diseases	11,978

Barrels of refuse and rag picker at West Broadway, detail, *Frank Leslie's Illustrated Newspaper*, April 23, 1881

opposite: Chart adapted from "Mortality Returns for the Year 1870 in the City of New-York—Facts Worth Knowing," *New York Times*, November 8, 1872

In some ways, the rise of the song broadside in mid-19th century urban America represents a democratization of the ballad tradition. Scholar Leslie Sheppard has written that "the printed ballad sheet must have contributed largely to the downfall of ancient traditional balladry in favor of new popular street songs. Who would pay a minstrel to sing long, old-fashioned ballads of far-off times when you could buy a smart, up-to-date broadside for a penny?"

Satire is used to bring attention to the dangers of milk in the mid-19th century in the songs "Swill Milk" and "Swill Milk #2." Written circa 1860 by anonymous authors, these songs chronicle one of New York's most troubling public health issues.

THE
SWILL MILK
SONG.

Air—"A Life on the Ocean Wave."

By BRICK-BAT.

Hurrah! for the steaming swill,
That flows from the seething still,
'Tis as pure as the gushing rill,
And my pockets with gold 'twill fill

CHORUS.

Hurrah! for the steaming swill,
That flows from the seething still,
'Tis as pure as the gushing rill,
And my pockets with gold 'twill fill.

Hurrah! for the steaming swill,
There's death in its sickning smell,
Like poison, 'tis sure to kill,
As a thousand tongues can tell

Oh if over the river you'll sail,
Or ride up town on a rail,
You may see me fill my pail,
From the cow without any tail.

Each morn as I stop at your door,
And sing my shrill "Yo ho!"
Just think where I was before
The roosters began to crow.

H ah! for the steaming swill
That bubbles in fiendish glee
From the vat in the poison mill,
'Tis richer than richness can be.

'Twill make the well one ill,
'Twill pale the cheek of health,
But Suffolk, Kings, Queens, Westchester, Fairfield,
Orange and Dutchess
County Pure Milk of the still,
Is one of our sources of wealth.

Andrews, Printer, 38 Chatham St. N.Y.

The Swill Milk Song, **song broadside, 1860**

PUBLIC HEALTH SINCE THE 1860S

It may have been no coincidence that the publishing house of John Andrews, who printed the Swill Milk songs, was located on Chatham Street in the heart of the notorious Five Points — a neighborhood that undoubtedly witnessed the toll that swill milk took on poor and working-class New Yorkers.

Adulterated and contaminated milk in those years was a huge health risk to city populations, especially to infants, and was linked to marasmus, scrofula, debilitating diarrheal diseases, typhoid, and scarlet fever. Unrefrigerated during the two- or three-day trip from rural dairy farm to urban market, shipped and stored in open containers, milk was vulnerable to spoiling and adulteration by farmers, shippers, dealers, and peddlers. Each year, for decades, hundreds of infants died from diseases that stemmed from their drinking bacteria-ridden, dirty, spoiled, and adulterated cow's milk.

In the 1860s, when 97 Orchard Street was built, diseases such as cholera, diphtheria, and infant diarrhea, all related to unsanitary conditions in the neighborhood, plagued the residents of the building. By the early 20th century, improvements in sanitation, health care, and knowledge about germs reduced the prevalence of these diseases among the children of 97 Orchard Street.

Indeed, by the early 20th century, New York had the lowest infant mortality rate of any city in the nation — the result of advances made in sanitation, the inauguration of municipal infant health clinics, and the advent of visiting home nurses. Surprisingly, in an almost complete reversal of the 19th century trend, infant mortality among native-born Americans had

"Milk and Its Adulteration: Early Morning Inspection," *Harper's Weekly Magazine*, 1882

surpassed that of foreign-born immigrants in New York. Throughout the late 19th century, public health initiatives in New York — from the introduction of pure drinking water to regular trash collection — sought to clean up the urban environment to prevent it from being a source of disease.

By the turn of the 20th century, responsibility for enforcing public health policy was expanded to include municipal departments other than the Board of Health, which had been founded in 1867. When the Tenement House Act became law in the same year, responsibility for enforcing it fell to Board of Health officials. By 1901, enforcement was under the purview of the Tenement House Department. Other public health initiatives such as street cleaning, medical inspection, and health education, once the responsibility of the Board of Health, also were placed in the hands of separate municipal departments.

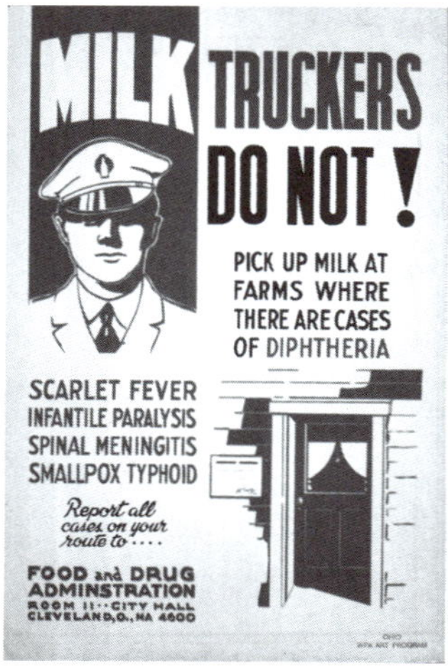

"Milk Truckers Do Not! Pick Up Milk at Farms Where There Are Cases of Diphtheria, Scarlett Fever, Infantile Paralysis, Spinal Meningitis, Smallpox, Typhoid," poster, Works Projects Administration, 1940

"Keep Your Fire Escapes Clear," poster produced by the Works Progress Administration for the New York City Tenement House Department, 1937

Though the Tenement House Department continued to enforce the requirements of the 1901 Tenement House Act — in February 1930, 97 Orchard Street resident Annie Katz was fined $10 by the Department for an illegal encumbrance on her apartment's fire escape — the long-term safety and survival of the Katz children was the result, in part, of a new, preventive approach to public health. Armed with the knowledge that germs and microorganisms cause disease, Department of Health officials embarked on a health education program to teach residents how to both prevent and detect early signs of illness.

According to school records, during the Spring semester of 1933, Jennie Katz was a twelve-year-old fifth grader at nearby Public School 42. There, this new approach to public health ensured that Jennie received more than instruction in reading, writing, and arithmetic. In cooperation with the Department of Health, beginning in the 1920s, New York's schools incorporated daily hygiene inspections and instruction.

An emphasis was placed on dental health and hygiene. Circulating around the classroom, the teacher, Miss Steiner, was instructed to ask her students, "How many have used a toothbrush this morning?" and, "How many own individual toothbrushes?" Throughout the year, teachers were expected to encourage their students to pay regular visits to a dentist.

Teachers of grade 1A were expected to cultivate a health-conscious pupil who developed the habit of "clearing the nostrils properly." Indeed, the daily hygiene inspection included scrutiny of the children's handkerchiefs. As the teacher walked around the classroom, the children were to "raise right hands with handkerchiefs in palm" while the teacher noted the presence and cleanliness of the handkerchiefs.

The idea that you could teach immigrants and their children to practice proper hygiene signaled a profound change in the way society viewed the relationship among ethnicity, class, and disease. Eighty years earlier, when the Moores lived at 97 Orchard Street, disease was poorly understood and immigrants were believed to be predisposed to unsanitary and unhealthy conditions because of their ethnic background.

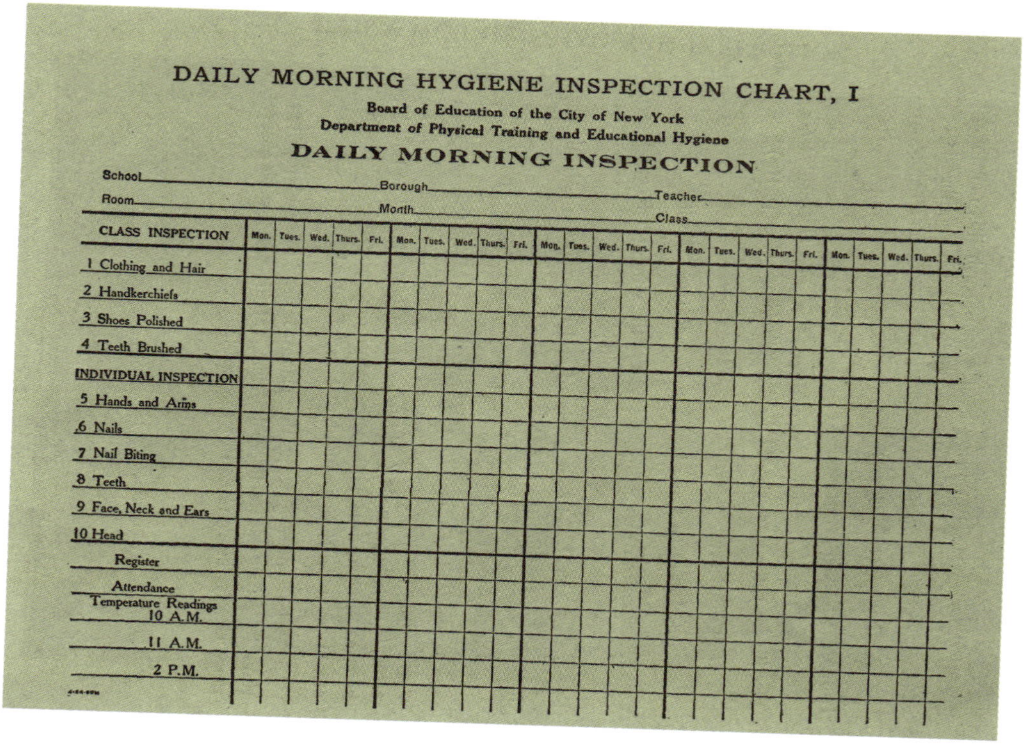

DAILY MORNING HYGIENE INSPECTION CHART, I

Board of Education of the City of New York
Department of Physical Training and Educational Hygiene

DAILY MORNING INSPECTION

School________ Borough________ Teacher________
Room________ Month________ Class________

CLASS INSPECTION	Mon.	Tues.	Wed.	Thurs.	Fri.	Mon.	Tues.	Wed.	Thurs.	Fri.	Mon.	Tues.	Wed.	Thurs.	Fri.	Mon.	Tues.	Wed.	Thurs.	Fri.	Mon.	Tues.	Wed.	Thurs.	Fri.
1 Clothing and Hair																									
2 Handkerchiefs																									
3 Shoes Polished																									
4 Teeth Brushed																									
INDIVIDUAL INSPECTION																									
5 Hands and Arms																									
6 Nails																									
7 Nail Biting																									
8 Teeth																									
9 Face, Neck and Ears																									
10 Head																									
Register																									
Attendance																									
Temperature Readings 10 A.M.																									
11 A.M.																									
2 P.M.																									

"Daily Hygiene Inspection Chart," Course of Study & Syllabus in Health Education for Elementary Schools Grade 1A-8B, New York City Board of Education, 1930

In 1933, almost 80 years after the songs "Swill Milk No. 1" and "Swill Milk No. 2" decried the dangers of drinking adulterated and contaminated cow's milk, New York's public schools distributed a Board of Health pamphlet that sang the praises of milk for a healthy diet. Addressed to mothers and fathers, the pocket-sized pamphlet began, "For good health, MILK should be in the diet of every man, woman, and child."

By the early 1930s, almost a century's worth of pure milk campaigns had succeeded in making cow's milk a safe and plentiful food for infants, children, and adults.

Diseases suffered by the Moore family no longer pose a threat to most Americans, but health issues are still a vital concern for immigrants. In New York City, immigrants report their health as poor more frequently than native-born New Yorkers. In addition, compared with U.S. citizens, recent immigrants are less likely to have health insurance or a primary-care physician, and are more prone to use hospital emergency rooms as their principal health provider. Surprisingly, even with less access to health care, immigrants are healthier by many measures than those born in the U.S. For example, they have less infant mortality and obesity, higher birth weights, and fewer new HIV diagnoses. The reasons for this are unclear. It is possible that immigrants are healthier than those who remain in their home countries and that this self selection could account for immigrants being more healthy relative to the entire U.S. population.

Why is it important to understand the connections between public health and the health of immigrants? In New York City, where nearly half the adult population is foreign born, the health of all immigrants increasingly characterizes the health of the community as a whole.

Today, 97 Orchard Street still stands as a Museum—a testament to the lives of the Moores and so many others who helped shape New York and America in the decades and centuries since their arrival.

MUNI METER
PAY &

IN MEMORY OF NUALA O'FAOLAIN

JOSEPH O'CONNOR was born in Dublin. Among his books are the novels *Cowboys And Indians* (shortlisted for the Whitbread Prize), *Desperadoes*, *The Salesman and Inishowen*, and the collection of short stories *True Believers*. His novel *Star of the Sea*, a story of Irish famine-era migration to the United States, was an international bestseller, selling more than a million copies and winning the Prix Littéraire Européen Zepter for best European novel of the year. Its sequel *Redemption Falls* received rave reviews internationally. *The Guardian* pronounced it 'A major work of modern fiction from an astonishingly accomplished writer' while *The Irish Times* called it 'A superb artistic achievement that deepens Joseph O'Connor's stature as a major novelist.' In 2004 he was awarded a Cullman Fellowship at the New York Public Library.

THE MOORES – AN IRISH FAMILY IN AMERICA is funded in part by Anglo Irish Bank; David Berg Foundation; City of New York Department of Cultural Affairs; Con Edison; The Richard H. Driehaus Foundation; Sarita Kennedy East Foundation; Emigrant Savings Bank; National Endowment for the Humanities; Historic Sites Fund of the National Trust for Historic Preservation; National Trust for Historic Preservation; New York Council for the Humanities, a state affiliate of the National Endowment for the Humanities; New York State Office of Parks, Recreation and Historic Preservation; a Cynthia Woods Mitchell Fund for Historic Interiors grant from the National Trust for Historic Preservation; Lower Manhattan Development Corporation/U.S. Department of Housing and Urban Development; and Save America's Treasures, a public-private partnership between the National Park Service and the National Trust for Historic Preservation.

front cover: "Emigrants Leaving Queenstown for New York," ***Harper's Weekly Magazine*****, 1874**

inside front cover: 1870 U.S. Census for 224 Elizabeth Street listing the Moore Family. The Moores moved to this building right after leaving 97 Orchard Street.

inside back cover: 1869 New York City Directory listing Joseph P. Moore at 97 Orchard Street.

Photographs:
All images in the collection of the Lower East Side Tenement Museum, except
pages 2, 6: Greg Scaffidi
pages 17, 43, 52, 60: Library of Congress
pages 35, 40-41: Angela Voulangas
page 53: Municipal Archives of the City of New York

Design and additional research by Angela Voulangas

ISBN: 978-0-9818412-0-5

TENEMENT MUSEUM

LOWER EAST SIDE TENEMENT MUSEUM
91 ORCHARD STREET, NEW YORK, NY 10002
212 431-0233